*For Niki and Nelli — N L*

*For Noah, Levi, Isaac, Daniel, Dylan and Jacob xxxxxx — J C*

Text copyright © Norbert Landa 2011
Illustrations copyright © Jane Chapman 2011
Original edition published in English by Little Tiger Press,
an imprint of Magi Publications, London, England, 2011
LTP/1400/0143/1010 • Printed in China

Library of Congress Cataloging-in-Publication Data
Landa, Norbert.
The slurpy burpy bear / Norbert Landa ; [illustrations by] Jane Chapman.
    p. cm.
Summary: Big Bear, always alone, likes that he can
slurp his soup, burp, and make other noises, not
realizing that the rabbits across the river think
the loud noises and odors are coming from a monster.
ISBN 978-1-56148-714-1 (hardcover : alk. paper)
[1. Etiquette--Fiction. 2. Bears--Fiction. 3. Rabbits--Fiction.
4. Friendship--Fiction.]  I. Chapman, Jane, 1970- ill. II. Title.
            PZ7.L23165Slu 2011
            [E]--dc22
            2010031233

# The Slurpy Burpy Bear

Norbert Landa          Jane Chapman

Good Books

Intercourse, PA 17534, 800/762-7171, www.GoodBooks.com

Big Bear noisily slurped his mushroom stew. He happily chomped and burped. "It's good to be the One and Only Bear!" he thought. "I can eat the way I like!"

# CRUNCH! CHOMP! BURP!

Across the river Little Rabbit's ears twitched. What was that terrible, crunching, roaring sound?

"Hush!" Mama Rabbit whispered. "That is the Beast's horrible sound!"

# SLURP! YUM YUM!

"The Beast?" Little Rabbit asked.
"Oh, yes!" Uncle Rabbit said
fearfully. "The Beast—with its
beastly paws and frightful fangs!"
"And HUGE eerie ears!"
Aunt Rabbit added.
"We all must hush and hide!"
Papa Rabbit told Little Rabbit,
"or the Beast will get us!"

Big Bear gulped down his
honey and had a last, big burp.
And as he got up, his bottom let
out a trumpy tune. Ooops!

Paaaaa

"The Beast is roaring! Hide, Little Rabbit!"
Papa Rabbit shrieked. "And hold your
breath—or you may faint from the
Beast's bad smell!"

Trembling, the rabbits hid in
their burrow.

arp!

Sometimes Big Bear thought of crossing the river to look for a friend. But he dipped his toes in the cold water and shivered. "Brrrr, brrrr, no way!"

Then he sang:

*"I am the One and Only,*
*The One and Only*
*Lonely Bear,*
*With no one there*
*for me to care . . ."*

And Big Bear couldn't help crying a little aloud.

Hooo sobb weee sobb wooaa

"It's the Beast's wicked howling again!" Little Rabbit whispered. "He is out on the hunt!"

One day, as Big Bear scratched against a big, old tree . . .

SNAP!

*Snap!* the tree cracked and fell across the river.

"I've built a bridge!" Big Bear said proudly. "Now I can look for a friend!" He brushed his fur and set off.

Across the river, Little Rabbit
chased butterflies in the woods.
"You'd better hide!" Little Rabbit
roared, "for I'm the Beast!"
Then suddenly . . .

# CRASH!

. . . Little Rabbit bumped into something big and soft and furry. From high above he heard a deep, friendly voice: "Hey, who's that down there?"

"I'm Little Rabbit,"
Little Rabbit said as strong
arms lifted him up.
"Oh, my! You are so big!"
"That's because I am Big Bear,"
Big Bear smiled. "Are there more
of you here?"
"Oh, yes!" Little Rabbit said.
"But we always hide from the Beast!"
"Beast?" Big Bear asked. "What Beast?"

Little Rabbit told Big Bear all about
the Beast's

roaring

and howling

and frightful fangs

and bad smell.

"Well, I've never seen any Beast,"
Big Bear said. "Perhaps I
could protect you."

"Oh, yes, please!"
Little Rabbit cheered.

So Big Bear carefully
put Little Rabbit on his
mighty shoulders, and
off they stomped.

Papa Rabbit nearly fell over in shock when he saw Little Rabbit. He knocked on Big Bear's belly.

"Don't you do Little Rabbit any
harm!" he cried.

"Don't worry, Papa!" Little Rabbit called.
"Big Bear is my friend. He has promised
to protect us from the Beast!"

"Can you really protect us?" Mama Rabbit asked.

"Yes, I can!" Big Bear answered with a smile. He let everyone feel his muscles and sit on his paws.

"Stay with us, Big Bear!" the rabbits cheered.

So Big Bear stayed, and soon the rabbits forgot all about the Beast. Only sometimes, faint sounds reminded them of something . . .

"You must never do this with others around you," Big Bear whispered to Little Rabbit.

And they giggled together. SLURP! SLURP! BURP!

As for Big Bear . . .

BUR

. . . he was so happy to no longer be
the One and Only Lonely Bear.
And when it was time to sleep,
he snuggled up with the rabbits and
sang to himself:

*"I am no longer lonely,*
*I am the Only*
*Big and Happy Bear.*
*My little friends may*
*slumber safe and sound,*
*Because they know*
*I'm always there."*